THE BOY WHO COUNTED STARS

THE BOY WHO COUNTED STARS

Poems by David L. Harrison
Illustrated by Betsy Lewin

WORDSONG
Boyds Mills Press

**To Jeff,
in lieu of a tiger
—D.L.H.**

**To Tom and Dan,
Dan'l and Holly,
and Dannee
—B.L.**

Text copyright © 1994 by David L. Harrison
Illustrations copyright © 1994 by Betsy Lewin
All rights reserved

Published by Wordsong
Boyds Mills Press, Inc.
A Highlights Company
815 Church Street
Honesdale, PA 18431
Printed in Mexico

Publisher Cataloging-in-Publication Data
Harrison, David L.
The boy who counted stars / poems by David L. Harrison ;
illustrated by Betsy Lewin.—1st ed.
[32]p. : col. ill. ; cm.
Summary : A collection of twenty-one poems to excite the imagination.
ISBN 1-56397-125-9
1. Children's poetry, American. [1. American poetry.]
I. Lewin, Betsy, ill. II. Title.
811.54—dc20   1994
Library of Congress Catalog Card Number 92-61632

First edition, 1994
Book designed by Charlotte Staub
The text of this book is set in 14-point Clarendon.
The illustrations are done in watercolors.
Distributed by St. Martin's Press

10   9   8   7   6   5   4   3   2   1

CONTENTS

WHERE CHILDREN GO

Far away and long ago
Is a secret place children know
Where fearsome fiery dragons roam
And magic forests grow.
Trolls dwell there,
Giants, too,
Witches boil their midnight brew,
And fairies bathe in morning dew
In the place that children know.

Grown-ups never seem to know
The secret place where children go
Where valiant warriors draw their swords
Against a wicked foe,
Where eagles speak
And spiders scold,
Enchanted streams run dark and cold,
And goblins bury hoards of gold
In the place that children know.

Follow me and we will go
Where banners fly and trumpets blow
To meet with elves in hidden glens
Where secret campfires glow,
Where wizards quarrel
And fairies tease
With merry voices on the breeze
And castles rise above the trees,
And only children know.

NEVER TALK TO PLANTS

You said,
If I talked to my plants,
They'd grow,
So I talked and talked,
And,
As you know,
They grew so high
They cracked the sky,
And a piece of it dropped
And fell in my eye,
Now my sister
And brother
And dog
Look blue,
All because
Of my plants
And you.

THE TROUBLE WITH MY HOUSE

I haven't any windows
And I haven't any doors,
I haven't any ceilings
And I haven't any floors,
I haven't got an attic
And I haven't any halls,
I haven't got a basement
And I haven't any walls,
I haven't got a roof
And that's the reason, I suppose,
Why rain keeps pouring on my head
And dripping off my nose.

MONSTER MANNERS

✕

When you meet a monster,
Don't waste your breath saying,
"How do you do?"
or
"Do you think it will rain?"
or
"How is your mother?"
Just say,
"I'm pleased to meet you."
'Cause monsters know,
When someone says,
"I'm pleased to meet you,"
That it's bad manners
For them
To eat you.

A BRIEF ROMANCE

"Oh Mistress Hen,
Won't you let me in?"
The fox asked
With a foxy grin,
But the hen said, "I'm too clever."

"I love you so,"
He murmured low,
"Just one little squeeze,
And then I'll go,"
But the hen just cackled, "Never!"

"Don't make me blue,
My sweet Baboo,
I'd do anything
For you,"
But the hen said, "No you wouldn't."

"My knees are weak,
I can scarcely speak,
I long to kiss
Your lovely beak,"
And the hen said, "I just couldn't."

He winked and smiled,
"My darling child,
I'll only stay
A little while,"
And the hen said, "We really shouldn't."

At last the hen
Let the fox come in,
And no one knows
What happened then,
Though it only took a minute.

I can only say,
When she hopped away,
Her tummy was round
And it made her sway,
And I think the fox was in it.

SALLY

Sally licked a light socket,
I can't imagine why,
I'm sure you can guess
That her hair's a mess,
But you ought to see her fly!

THE BOY WHO COUNTED STARS

Jimmy decided, when he was seven,
That he would count the stars in heaven.
"Counting them all," he said, "will be fun,
And I'll never give up till I'm done."

"You cannot count them all," said his dad,
"It's too big a job for a little lad."
But Jimmy said, "I've already begun,
And I'll never give up till I'm done."

"Come in!" called his mother. "It's time for bed."
But Jimmy counted stars instead,
And, when it was morning and too light to see,
He'd counted twelve thousand and three.

Night after night he was back in the yard.
"Counting stars," he said, "isn't hard,
I'm already up to one million and one,
And I'll never give up till I'm done."

A year rolled by, and Jimmy was eight.
He slept all day and stayed up late.
"Give up!" begged his father. "This simply won't do!"
But Jimmy said, "I'm not through."

By the time he was twenty he'd counted a billion.
The day he turned forty he shouted, "One trillion!"
His dad said, "You'll never get finished, my son,
If you live to one hundred and one."

"The neighbors are talking," his mother sighed,
But Jimmy just smiled with quiet pride,
"I'm up to ten trillion, three billion and two,
And you know I'll not stop till I'm through."

When Jimmy was eighty, he said, with a grin,
"I've counted three quadrillion billion and ten.
My life counting stars has been wonderfully nice,
But I wish I could count them all twice!"

Jim was one hundred one when he died,
And he wasn't quite finished, but oh how he'd tried!
The neighbors were sad and felt sorry for Jim.
They knew what finishing the job meant to him.

But suddenly they heard a voice in the sky,
"I know I can count the last star if I try!
Ninety-nine jillion zillion trillion and two!
I've done it! I'm finally through!"

"At last he has finished his job!" people said,
"Now he can rest his weary old head."
But again they could hear Jimmy chuckle with glee,
"From up here the stars are much easier to see.
I think I will count them again just for fun."
And they all heard him shout, "That's one!"

HOW WILLY GREW

Willy was smaller than the other boys,
But his mother said, "Son, don't fret,
One of these days you'll grow a foot,
You'll catch those big boys yet."
And sure enough, Willy grew a foot,
But not like his mother said,
'Cause whatever it was had five little toes,
And it stuck right out of his head.

THEY

I don't know their names,
But They live in the grass,
And They're only two inches tall,
And nobody knows where They came from
Or why They're so terribly small.
They slip through the clover
And hide in the leaves
So you seldom can see them at all,
And nobody knows why They live there
Near the base of our garden wall.
They dance and parade
By the light of the moon
And visit with crickets all day,
And nobody knows how They got there
Or whether They're planning to stay.
And maybe you'll meet them,
And maybe you won't,
If you come to my house to play,
'Cause everyone wants to know who They are
But nobody knows but They.

HARE ON THE STAIR

A bear with no hair
Met a hare on the stair.
"Dear Hare," said the bear who was bare,
"I have nothing to wear."

The hare only stared
At the bear who was bare.
"Stay there," said the hare with a glare,
"You cannot wear my hair."

The bear took the hare
With the hair up the stair,
And when they were finished up there,
'Twas the hare who was bare.

THE PERFECT DIET

Mrs. LaPlump weighed 300 pounds
And her husband weighed 202.
"I've got to lose some weight," she said,
"I'll give up potatoes and pizza and bread,"
And Mr. LaPlump said, "I will, too,
My darling, I'll do it for you."

So each of them lost 100 pounds
And he only weighed 102.
"I've got to lose more weight," she said.
"This next 100," said he, "I dread,
For when we are finished I'll only weigh 2,
But darling, I'll do it for you."

So they lost another 100 pounds
And her figure was perfect and trim,
But there is a lesson here I think
'Cause Mr. LaPlump continued to shrink
Till one day he disappeared down the sink,
And you may find that grim, my dears,
But that was the end of him.

SOMEBODY CALL THE DOCTOR

"Sit up and cut your food," we said.
"Wolfing it down is rude," we said.
"There's gravy all over your chin," we said.
"You finish before we begin," we said.
"You don't even know what you're eating," we said.
"You act like you're late for a meeting," we said.
"You don't seem to understand," we said.
"Someone could lose a hand," we said.
"You don't even bother to chew," we said.
"You really weren't born in a zoo," we said.
Now I think we should call the doctor,
I hope it's not too late,
Won't somebody call the doctor?
Jeffrey just swallowed his plate.

THE RACE

When a snail races,
He wears a saddle
(The same as a horse),
And he carries a jockey
(The same as a horse),
And the track is a quarter mile
(The same for a horse),
But no matter how fast
A snail runs the course,
Here's a tip—
(Bet on the horse).

WEEDS

Said Mrs. Towers to Mr. Reeds,
"Why do you water those wretched weeds?"
Said Mr. Reeds, "Well, don't you know
That blue-ribbon weeds need water to grow?"
Said Mrs. Towers to Mr. Reeds,
"I'll give you some blue-ribbon flower seeds
If you'll promise to pull those weeds and make room
For lovely blue-ribbon flowers to bloom."
Said Mr. Reeds, with a rasping wheeze,
"Flowers make me sniff and sneeze,
So I yank them up and throw them out
To give my weeds more room to sprout."
And he said with pride, "As you can see,
No one grows better weeds than me.
I'll never waste my time on flowers,"
Said Mr. Reeds to Mrs. Towers.
And I'm sure you know that Mr. Reeds
Won ten blue ribbons for his champion weeds.

WHAT I'D LIKE TO BE

I'd like to be a butterfly!
> *A butterfly?*

A butterfly.
I'd like to be a butterfly and live among the flowers.
Boys and girls would follow me.
> *Follow you?*

Follow me.
Boys and girls would wave their nets and follow me for hours.
> *What if they should capture you?*

Capture me?
> *Capture you!*
> *What if they should capture you and pin you in a box?*

Well . . . then . . . I'd . . . like to be a boy again.
> *A boy again?*

A boy again.
I'd like to be a boy again, unless I were a fox!
I'd like to be a wily fox!
> *A wily fox?*

A wily fox.
I'd like to be a wily fox and chase the farmer's chickens.
Every night I'd steal a hen.
> *You'd steal a hen?*

I'd steal a hen.

I'd grab the plumpest, juiciest hen and dash off like the dickens!

What if the farmer shot at you?

Shot at me?

Shot at you!

What if the farmer shot at you and blasted off your tail?

Well . . . then . . . I'd . . . like to be a boy again.

A boy again?

A boy again.

I'd like to be a boy again, unless I were a snail!

I'd like to be a garden snail.

A garden snail?

A garden snail.

I'd like to be a garden snail and carry my house around.

I'd take all day to move an inch.

You'd take all day?

To move an inch.

I'd take all day to move an inch and I'd never make a sound.

What if the gardener picked you up?

Picked me up?

Picked you up!

What if the gardener picked you up and served you with his tea?

Well . . . then . . . I'd . . . like to be a boy again.

A boy again?

A boy again.

I'd like to be a boy again.

There's nothing I'd rather be.

MY DINOSAUR

I caught a dinosaur
And taught him to quack
And sit up and beg
And roll on his back
And I taught him to curtsy
And he gave me a rose
And I polished his scales
And painted his toes
And I taught him to talk
And we gossiped all day
And he said, "I'm hungry,"
And I offered him hay
And he said, "I'd rather
Nibble off your ear,"
And I said, "You'd better
Get out of here,"
And if you think I'm lyin'
I dare you to find
A dinosaur around here
Of any kind.

THE ARGUMENT

A slug and a snail
Met by chance
On a garden wall,
For eleven days
They blinked and nodded
But that was all
Until at last
The snail felt strangely
Moved to speak,
"Morning," she said,
And the slug just nodded
For another week,
Then one night
He spoke right up,
"Evening," he said,
The snail considered
For nearly a month
While her face turned red,
"All this bickering,"
She said, "is more
Than I can bear,"
She left the wall
But as far as I know
The slug's still there.

ELEPHANT RULES

Never be silly or mean
To an elephant,
Never feed chili or beans
To an elephant,
Never go near
To the front or the rear
Of a chilifull, bellyfull
Smellyphant.

BUILT KIND OF FUNNY

Jeremy Money is
Built kind of funny as
Everyone knows when he
Goes down the street,
Jeremy Money is
Built kind of funny he
Runs with his nose and he
Smells with his feet.

TEACHING BABY

As Baby sipped from the garden hose,
Brother turned it on,
I winked and hollered, "Thar she blows!"
And presto! She was gone!
"Look at her go!" we cried with glee,
"She must be ten miles high!"
We're just as proud as we can be
That Baby learned to fly.

BEDTIME

"Read me a story,
Please read me to sleep."
"What kind of story, my love?"
"Of raindrops and rainbows
And furry soft kittens
And ponies and gentle white doves."

"Read me a story,
Please read me to sleep."
"What kind of story, my sweet?"
"Of magical castles
And harps that can sing
And gypsies who dance in the street."

"Read me a story,
Please read me to sleep."
"What kind of story, my pet?"
"Of pirates and treasure
And ships in the night
And mermaids who escape from a net."

"Read me a story,
Please read me to sleep."
"What kind of story, my child?"
"Of mountains and meadows
And bubbling brooks
And stallions who run free and wild."

"Read me a story,
Please read me to sleep."
"But what kind of story, my dear?"
"Read any story
And I'll go to sleep,
As long as I know you are near."